Birthday Beastie

ALL ABOUT COUNTING

Written by Kirsten Hall

Illustrated by Bev Luedecke

children's press®

A Division of Scholastic Inc.

New York   Toronto   London   Auckland   Sydney
Mexico City   New Delhi   Hong Kong
Danbury, Connecticut

About the Author

Kirsten Hall, formerly an early-childhood teacher,
is a children's book editor in New York City. She has been
writing books for children since she was thirteen years old
and now has over sixty titles in print.

About the Illustrator

Bev Luedecke enjoys life and nature in Colorado.
Her sparkling personality and artistic flair are reflected in her
creation of Beastieville, a world filled with lovable Beasties
that are sure to delight children of all ages.

Library of Congress Cataloging-in-Publication Data

Hall, Kirsten.
  Birthday Beastie : all about counting / written by Kirsten Hall ;
illustrated by Bev Luedecke.
      p. cm.
Summary: Bee-Bop has a wonderful time at his birthday party.
  ISBN 0-516-22891-9 (lib. bdg.)   0-516-24651-8 (pbk.)
  [1. Birthdays–Fiction. 2. Parties–Fiction. 3. Counting. 4. Stories in
rhyme.] I. Luedecke, Bev, ill. II. Title.
  PZ8.3.H146Bi 2003
  [E]–dc21
                              2003001587

A NOTE TO PARENTS AND TEACHERS

Welcome to the world of the Beasties, where learning is FUN. In each of the charming stories in this series, the Beasties deal with character traits that every child can identify with. Each story reinforces appropriate concept skills for kindergartners and first graders, while simultaneously encouraging problem-solving skills. Following are just a few of the ways that you can help children get the most from this delightful series.

Stories to be read and enjoyed

Encourage children to read the stories aloud. The rhyming verses make them fun to read. Then ask them to think about alternate solutions to some of the problems that the Beasties have faced or to imagine alternative endings. Invite children to think about what they would have done if they were in the story and to recall similar things that have happened to them.

Activities reinforce the learning experience

The activities at the end of the books offer a way for children to put their new skills to work. They complement the story and are designed to help children develop specific skills and build confidence. Use these activities to reinforce skills. But don't stop there. Encourage children to find ways to build on these skills during the course of the day.

Learning opportunities are everywhere

Use this book as a starting point for talking about how we use reading skills or math or social studies concepts in everyday life. When we search for a phone number in the telephone book and scan names in alphabetical order or check a list, we are using reading skills. When we keep score at a baseball game or divide a class into even-numbered teams, we are using math.

The more you can help children see that the skills they are learning in school really do have a place in everyday life, the more they will think of learning as something that is part of their lives, not as a chore to be borne. Plus you will be sending the important message that learning is fun.

Madeline Boskey Olsen, Ph.D.
Developmental Psychologist

Bee-Bop

Puddles

Slider

Pip &Zip

Wilbur

Flippet

Pooky

Mr. Rigby

We're
the
Beasties

Smudge

Toggles

Bee-Bop wakes up feeling happy.
He will feel like this all day!

He will have a birthday party.
Ten good friends are on their way.

Bee-Bop has to set the table.
He has eleven nice plates and spoons.

He has eleven new forks and glasses.
He has nine big round balloons!

Bee-Bop makes eleven cookies.
Then he puts them in to bake.

They smell good! They look good, too!
Now he makes one birthday cake.

"Hi there, Toggles! Hi there, Flippet!
Hi there, Wilbur, Zip, and Pip."

Everyone is here to party.
Flippet does a birthday flip!

Zip and Pip now light the candles.
"Happy birthday!" sing the friends.

Bee-Bop loves his birthday party.
He hopes that it never ends.

Bee-Bop gets so many presents.
Each starts with the letter B!

Bee-Bop feels so very happy.
"Are these presents all for me?"

Zip and Pip each hold one present.
Each is flat and each is square.

"Did you get me books?" asks Bee-Bop.
"I will read them over there!"

Mr. Rigby gives one present.
"It can sail and it can float!"

Bee-Bop claps his hands together.
Bee-Bop thinks it is a boat.

Wilbur gives Bee-Bop one present.
"This is for your messy room!"

Bee-Bop thinks this gift is funny.
"Wilbur gave me a big broom!"

Pooky gives Bee-Bop one present.
Bee-Bop asks, "Is it a toy?"

"No," says Pooky. "Open it!"
Bee-Bop loves the little boy.

"Will you open mine now, Bee-Bop?"
Bee-Bop tells big Smudge, "Okay!"

"This must be a ball!" says Bee-Bop.
Smudge says, "Right! Now we can play!"

Bee-Bop looks at all his presents.
He is glad his friends are here!

Bee-Bop loves his birthday party.
Birthdays should be twice a year!

PARTY COUNT

1. How many friends are in this picture?

2. How many cookies can you count?

3. How many different hats do you see?

SOUNDS LIKE...

The word "true" sounds a lot like "blue." What other words can you think of that sound like "blue"?

LET'S TALK ABOUT IT

Everyone loves presents!

1. What are some of the best gifts you've ever given?

2. Have you ever made a gift for someone? What was it?

3. You don't have to wait for a holiday to give a gift. What are some other times when it's nice to give someone a present?

WORD LIST

a	eleven	hold	over	the
all	ends	hopes	party	their
and	everyone	I	Pip	them
are	feel	in	plates	then
asks	feels	is	play	there
at	feeling	it	Pooky	these
bake	flat	letter	present	they
ball	flip	light	presents	thinks
balloons	Flippet	like	puts	this
be	float	little	read	to
Bee-Bop	for	look	Rigby	together
big	forks	looks	right	Toggles
birthday	friends	loves	room	too
birthdays	funny	makes	round	toy
boat	gave	many	sail	twice
books	get	me	says	up
boy	gets	messy	set	very
broom	gift	mine	should	wakes
cake	gives	Mr.	sing	way
can	glad	must	smell	we
candles	glasses	never	Smudge	Wilbur
claps	good	new	so	will
come	hands	nice	spoons	with
comes	happy	no	square	year
cookies	has	now	starts	you
day	have	okay	table	your
did	he	on	tells	Zip
does	here	one	ten	
each	his	open	that	